NICK
OF
TIME

NICK
OF
TIME

A Nick Donahue Adventure

CATHI STOLER

First published by Level Best Books 2023

Copyright © 2023 by Cathi Stoler

All rights reserved. No part of this publication may be reproduced, stored or transmitted in any form or by any means, electronic, mechanical, photocopying, recording, scanning, or otherwise without written permission from the publisher. It is illegal to copy this book, post it to a website, or distribute it by any other means without permission.

This novel is entirely a work of fiction. The names, characters and incidents portrayed in it are the work of the author's imagination. Any resemblance to actual persons, living or dead, events or localities is entirely coincidental.

Cathi Stoler asserts the moral right to be identified as the author of this work.

Author Photo Credit: Oskar Martinez

First edition

ISBN: 978-1-68512-357-4

Cover art by Level Best Designs

This book was professionally typeset on Reedsy.
Find out more at reedsy.com

To Sue Rafaj

Praise of Nick of Time

"Come along for a dangerous, exciting ride with Nick Donahue, professional gambler, as he's caught in a whole new game with all the wrong people. It takes sharp wits and a cool head, and some flashes of humor, to find his way out before he has to turn in all his chips."—Triss Stein, author of the Erica Donato Mysteries

"In this fast-paced thriller, Cathi Stoler intertwines suspense and violence with just enough dark humor to keep the entertainment level on extra-high."—Terrie Farley Moran, author of the Murder She Wrote mysteries

"A good-looking gambler, an intriguing mystery, and the suspense of the chase. This book has all the ingredients for a great read, and it's short and sweet. I loved Nick. Is there anything better than a bad boy who's a good guy?"—Leigh Neeley, author of *Healing Magic*

"*Nick Of Time* is fast, fizzy, and most of all, fun. With breakneck speed, gambler Nick Donohue's adventures take him down a twisty path filled with high stakes risks and increasingly improbable rewards. Nick's cheeky sense of humor never deserts him, even when his luck seems to have run out, but he's not the kind of guy to give up without a fight. Love and loss play a role, along with suspense and deceit, and as Nick prepares to make the wager of a lifetime, the odds are good the reader will win big."—Lori Robbins, author of the On Pointe Mystery series

Praise for The Murder On The Rocks Mysteries

BAR NONE

"Cathi Stoler's *Bar None* is a New York crime novel with a modern twist—dark, deadly and loaded with memorable characters. Sidle up to the bar and order a few rounds of this smooth, potent drink. You won't regret it."—Alex Segura, author of the Anthony Award-nominated Pete Fernandez Mystery series

LAST CALL

"Evil lurks all around us and in *Last Call* Jude Dillane finds it right next to her when a New Year's Eve murder near her restaurant uncovers a link to past unsolved slayings. Fast-paced, well-plotted, with memorable characters, Cathi Stoler does not disappoint." — James L'Etoile, author of *Dead Drop*, A Detective Nathan Parker Novel

STRAIGHT UP

"Stoler serves up another round of 110-proof suspense in this engaging serial killer thriller. Well worth bending your elbow for."—Richie Narvaez, author of *Noiryorican*

WITH A TWIST

"Jude is back for another, truly exciting adventure-this time on the high seas! Packed full of shocking twists, a luxe cruise ship setting and intriguing characters, *With A Twist* is an escapist delight!"—Alison Gaylin, Edgar Award-winning (*USA Today* and international bestselling) author of *The Collective*

Chapter One

You would think that after being kidnapped, beaten senseless, and nearly murdered by a ruthless gang of Serbian jewel thieves, I'd have the good sense to stay away from anything remotely redolent of danger, but you would be wrong.

After the gang let me go—well, left me bound and gagged and tossed on the side of a treacherous mountain road in the middle of the night—I thought I might die anyway.

"Go back to America," one of the thugs whispered in my ear, his scratchy voice and garlicky breath enough to put me off shrimp scampi for a long time. "Leave the Czech Republic, Mr. Donahue, and don't ever come back." His take on a fond farewell before opening the van's door and rolling me out onto the road.

I hadn't heard my name pronounced with such venom or menace since the third-grade bully called me out in the schoolyard after I glued his lunchbox shut. My gag prevented me from explaining that I now lived in England, not America, but I got his message loud and clear. As loud as the bells and whistles on a slot machine announcing a really big payoff.

My face hit the roadway first, sliding along loose gravel, and felt like some deranged barber was intent on shaving off my skin as well as my beard. When I stopped rolling, I tried to catch my breath, took in a lungful of air, and realized it was freezing. My torn white dress shirt and black pants—the remains of the clothing I was wearing when the gang grabbed me—were not exactly the best options for a midnight stroll through the forest. As if the temperature weren't enough, it was also pitch-black, with no moon or stars to give me even a glimmer of what was in front of or behind me. Eventually, I stood and stumbled along, hoping a wild animal looking to nibble on a tasty gambler as a midnight snack wouldn't attack me.

Finally, after what seemed like hours, I managed to untie myself and remove the gag. I heard the rumble of a cranky engine in the distance, and when it got close enough, I flagged down a farm truck making an early morning run down the mountain. The driver of the truck, obviously abandoning any good sense he might have had, aimed his thumb toward the back and muttered something that sounded vaguely like Prague. Good enough for me. Sitting among his cabbages, I had time to reflect on my situation and on Marina, the woman who had first ensnared me, then ultimately saved me.

Chapter Two

I t had all started a little over a month ago in Venice, where I was touring the city's top casinos, trying to break the bank at each one.

Venice was the stuff of dreams: a city rising from the water, its sleek gondolas bobbing along the Grand Canal, ready to take you to the famous Harry's Bar and the most celebrated casinos. There were also the centuries-old palazzos, many of them crumbling and ready to be swept away by the tide. Kind of like I was feeling now, after Marina.

I'm Nick Donahue, citizen of the world, gambler by trade. Blackjack is my game. The odds favor the player, at least slightly, or so I've learned over the years. I travel from casino to casino, mostly in Europe, where I seem to have developed a reputation as a polished and sophisticated player. If you're thinking James Bond, get over it. It's not all Chemin de Fer, vodka martinis, and gorgeous women throwing themselves at me. At least it wasn't until Marina.

"*Buona fortuna,*" she purred into my ear as she leaned over my shoulder, her breast brushing my arm. She placed 500 euros next to mine on the green baize of the high stakes table at the Palazzo Ducale Casino. I had a Jack in the hole and pulled an up card of ten. The dealer had a ten showing and flipped over a four. He had to draw. Poor guy, it was an eight, which meant I won. And so did she. *"Grazie,"* she licked her lips as she swept up her winnings and drifted off into the Venetian night in a cloud of perfume that made me want to inhale forever.

A few more hands, and it was time to cash in. I'd had a good run and was up more than fifteen thousand euros. "For the boys," I said and knocked two 100-euro chips on the edge of the table and tossed them to the dealer, ignoring the scowl of the pit boss who tried to make me feel like I was stealing from his personal bank account. Amateur. I'd been stared down by better men than him, including my mother. I finished the Scotch I'd been drinking and left the casino. In the lobby, the lift pinged open and carried me to the penthouse suite the management had so graciously comped. A "Do Not Disturb" sign hung on the doorknob. I hadn't placed it there. Two fingers and the door swung open.

There she was, in my bed, the terry robe from the bath wrapped around her, looking even more luscious than she had in the casino.

"Ciao, Bello." Her voice was smooth as silk as she got up slowly, a flash of long, tanned legs diverting my attention. She reached for a bottle of Cristal that was already open and chilling beside her. *"Per te."*

I wondered briefly if the management had comped her, too. Their way of distracting me from my game. She rose from the bed and crossed to me slowly, the robe moving with her, revealing tantalizing glimpses of the tanned body beneath. She lifted her face to mine and waited for me to kiss her. I did, and all thoughts of the management were quickly forgotten.

During the night, I discovered the lady spoke perfect English, even if the words we used were not necessarily part of polite conversation. When I awoke shortly after dawn, she was gone, a folded piece of the hotel's stationery standing in for where her head had rested on the pillow. *"Meet me at 2 at Il Nino"* was all it said. My favorite *ristorante* in Venice served a dish I loved, *pasta alla bursara*. Not only had she seduced me—it hadn't been hard—but she also knew more about me than I liked. I folded the note and wondered if it was my rugged good looks or something else that was piquing her interest.

Il Nino tilted toward the water on a small side canal in the Cannaregio section where Venice's hordes of tourists rarely ventured. That was fine with Nino. He didn't want or need them and stationed a snarky-looking waiter by the entrance who discouraged *"I touristi"* with a barked-out *"chiuso"* in a tone that sent them scurrying down the cobblestone *"fondamenta"* faster than a *"ratto"* avoiding the city's pest control brigade.

An intimate place with discreet management, Il Nino had its regulars who appreciated the privacy as much as the food. Apparently, Marina was now one of them, if the bevy of waiters hovering at her table like seagulls waiting for scraps were any indication.

"Hello, there. Nice to see you again." I slid into the seat opposite hers and gave the staff my best 'screw off' smile.

Her soft laugh tinkled through the dining room as she cupped my chin in her hand and squeezed it the way a maiden aunt does to a small nephew. "No need to be jealous, Nick. We were just talking."

"It seems I'm at a disadvantage," I replied. "You know all about me." I ticked the items off on my fingers. Who I am. Where I gamble. Where I'm staying. What I like to do in bed. Even where I like to eat." My eyes took in the room, a cozy wood-paneled space with hand-blown Murano glass lamps hanging from the ceiling. "And I, on the other hand, well, I still don't know your name."

She lifted one eyebrow. "Oh, I think you learned a few things about me last night." She laughed, then continued, "I'm Marina. Marina DiPietro."

I sat back and gave her my best poker face while I considered the facts. I'd thought about why she'd come into my bed—I'm not that irresistible. I'd known right away that she wasn't a hooker, but she had to have had a reason. I was trying to decide whether or not to challenge her. DiPietro was as common in Italy as St. John in England or Smith in the States. I decided to let it go for now. "Okay. Marina DiPietro it is. Now that we got that out of the way, why don't you tell me what it is you want with me?"

And she did.

Chapter Three

I brought myself back to the present and shuddered. It might be hard to understand, but dire as it appeared right now, the present was no competition for the horror of the past few weeks. My body convulsed at the thought of what might have happened if Marina had abandoned me.

Believe me, there *are* a few fates worse than death. I'd been living one in a secluded villa high in the hills somewhere in the Czech Republic. A place where no one would have found me if anyone had actually cared to look.

My captors had gone easy at first—a black eye, split lip, sore ribs—no hanging from the ceiling or electrodes below the belt. But I knew that could change at any moment. The leader was too calm and too patient. And that scared me. I knew it was just a matter of time before the real work began. He'd expect me to fold. And why shouldn't I? Why the hell should I care what happened to the people who'd put me in a cold, damp cell? They knew you win some and you lose some. But me? If I'd lost this time, it would have been my life.

I understood it would be better to forget but I couldn't let go so easily. It all came flooding back over and over again, like a song you hear once and can't get out of your head for days.

Marina's story was a modern variation of the damsel in

distress theme. A tale of really bad guys doing very bad things with very big guns and a beautiful woman who needed rescuing.

She'd filled me in at Il Nino's over the *pasta alla bursara* and a bottle of the local vino. She was on assignment for Eurotec International, a global insurance company based in London. Her job was to track down a gang of Serbian jewel thieves who were knocking off high-end jewelry stores all across the continent. Their latest job had involved a smash and grab on the Via Veneto at Domani's, Rome's most expensive and exclusive jewelry store, and making off with a king's ransom in gems.

Eurotec had gotten a hot lead and their first big break: the leader of the crew, a short, stocky fellow nicknamed 'Clouseau,' had been traced to Venice and linked to Guillermo Gennaro, the general manager of the Palazzo Ducale Casino, which is where I came in. Eurotec had been looking for a way to infiltrate the gang. A mutual friend in government in London, Nigel Phillips, who knew I was in Venice, had suggested a desperate gambler losing big at the casino—me—might be just the ticket. I'd have to remember to thank him properly the next time we met.

"How did anyone come to that conclusion?" I queried. Nigel knew that for me, snorkeling was about as adventurous as it got. "I play Blackjack. I do *not* chase down dangerous jewel thieves. And, as you may have noticed, I'm not losing or desperate." Didn't she remember the chips she scooped up last night? I hoped I didn't sound like I was bragging or whining.

"But you will be," Marina had replied, "once you start to lose big and Gennaro sees the hole you're digging for yourself. You'll go to him for help. Act a little frantic, and try to get more credit. He'll recognize the opportunity and make you a deal.

"Look," she sighed, "Gennaro is the middleman, the one moving the goods. There's someone bigger behind all this, and that's who we're after." She shook her head. "These guys know every police force in Europe is looking for them. They've scored too many times. They know they have to find another way to move the gems."

She must have caught the "are you out of your mind" look on my face. "Don't worry, Nick, Eurotec security will be watching you every minute. You'll be perfectly safe."

Marina leaned in close and kept up the pitch. "Eurotec has paid out a fortune." She lowered her voice. "Honestly, one more heist like this could ruin them. They're desperate to catch Clouseau's crew and repatriate the gems. And so am I." She laid her hand over mine on the snowy white tablecloth. "If I don't close this case, I'm out."

I told you, damsel in distress. "I need to think about this." I didn't want to tell her how much I hated looking like a loser. I had my reputation to think of and my pride, not to mention my life.

"Let's go back to my hotel. There are a few things I want to show you." She took my hand and led me from the restaurant like a lamb to the slaughter. "Please, Nick, let me convince you."

You're right. She did.

Chapter Four

I 'd been playing at the posh Palazzo Ducale Casino in a canal-side palace near Santa Croce. In the three days since I met Marina, I'd gone from a winner to a beggar.

And now, here I was sitting in Guillermo Gennaro's ornately decorated office, humbly seeking funds to continue my losing streak. Looking around, I figured the casino must have been raking it in—or maybe it was Gennaro's extracurricular activities that paid for the overdone splendor.

Gennaro, who was tall, thin, and swarthy, must have fancied himself a modern-day version of one of the Venetian Doges, one of the Dukes in charge of the city a thousand years ago. He seemed to favor narrow-cut black silk suits with red or purple shirts and matching print cravats. Combined with antique hand-blown glass on nearly every surface, softly glowing sconces on the walls, and a king-size gilded desk as the office's centerpiece, his appearance gave the impression of being back in the fifteen hundreds, with me as the supplicant and he as the duke in his palace dispensing favors. The real Doge would probably have marched him across *"Il Ponte dei Sospiri,"* the Bridge of Sighs, and tossed him in the attached dungeon for the crime of preening.

It had been a whirlwind of losing thanks to my playing like a total neophyte—although losing wasn't as simple as you might think. I had to be extremely careful about just how badly I played, without creating too much suspicion. Systematically disposing of a small fortune provided by Eurotec International took skill and cunning—you'd be surprised at how quickly my chips found their way to the casino's vault. Well, the idea *was* to ingratiate myself as a loser in need of credit.

The bile rose in my throat every time I had to throw a hand. I had to choose my moments carefully, double up on pairs and take too many hits, or draw on a low card when the dealer had a low card showing—a must-draw situation for him—and hopefully take his break card. I'd act out the *"I had such a strong feeling I'd get the card I needed"* routine, then pretend to be devastated when it didn't work out. As you can imagine, playing like a total jerk-off didn't make me very popular with the other players at my table since my mistakes often cost them as well. Forget sympathy. They were ready to string me up.

My old friend, the pit boss, didn't take his beady eyes off me. He made it pretty obvious he thought something was going on but he couldn't figure out exactly what—I wasn't cheating or card counting. He kept peering down his long, Italian nose and rubbing his hands together in anticipation of catching me out. With each hand, I had to be as smooth and stealthy as a gigolo stalking his next rich widow. It was exhausting.

The only positive about the whole deal was Marina. We met in her room in the wee hours after I finished playing, and she fed me champagne and caviar, whispered encouraging words in my ear, and took me to bed. After our lovemaking, we'd talk about the next steps. I came to realize how smart and incisive she was. Nothing got by her. She had planned our strategy down to my, or Eurotec's, last euro.

I'd blown through about a hundred thousand of their money and Marina thought it was time to approach Gennaro. Now, here I was.

"So, Mr. Donahue," he inclined his head toward me, "you would like the casino to extend you credit? Hmmm. I see."

He actually said that the twit, putting his index finger up to his lips in what I imagined he thought of as a pensive pose.

"It is not our policy to give credit to any of the casino's patrons." Now, his shoulders shrugged upward like broken angel wings and his hands reached to the sky in an 'I'm so sorry gesture.' "There is nothing I can do. My hands are tied."

It was time to plead. "Signor Gennaro, please." I let my voice crack just a little, then went through the motions of pulling myself together. "I've been playing at your casino for years. As I explained, my personal funds are tied up right now." Marina and Eurotec had seen to that for me. "All I want is for the casino to extend me a line of credit for fifty thousand euros. If you check, you'll see I'm good for it." Bet he'd heard that one a million times. And when he did check, which I was pretty sure he would, it would appear that I was totally tapped out and probably lying through my teeth. "I'm just having a bad run at the moment. I'm sure that my luck will change and I'll be able to cover any credit easily."

He watched me carefully the whole time I spoke. I hope I had appeared just desperate enough to get his wheels turning.

"Mr. Donahue," he rose from behind his desk, "let me think about this. Perhaps there is a way I can help you."

I rose as well and extended my hand.

He shook it limply. "I'll be in touch. Good day."

The bastard made me wait an entire day before he got back

to me. I'd hung around the casino, playing a hand or two and trying to appear anxious, which wasn't too much of a stretch, when he finally summoned me back to his office.

He had decided to help me, he said, as a personal favor. The fifty thousand euros would be made available free and clear if I, in turn, would do a personal favor for him.

There was a small package that had to be delivered to Prague in the next few days. He needed someone he could trust implicitly to carry it for him, no questions asked. It was the quid pro quo for the money. I was sure he had checked on my finances and noted that I appeared to be not only broke but also very much in debt. If I was interested in his proposition, I was to leave on the late train from the Venezia Mestre station this evening and change in Rome for the fast train to the Czech Republic. If not, I would have to find the money elsewhere.

I cast my eyes down and slowly nodded yes, in a "what choice do I have" manner. We had a deal. I went back to my room to pack. I wouldn't be able to call Marina—I was sure Gennaro had people monitoring me, but hopefully, so was the crew from Eurotec. They would let her know I was on the move.

Chapter Five

I departed on the overnight express at 8:44 PM, and the train ride was uneventful, if a bit bumpy. As we passed through the Italian countryside in the gathering dusk, I tried to figure out which of the passengers might be my undercover shadows, but I had no luck with that and decided to get something to eat before retiring for the night.

I had a small collision with a young mother and her child on my way out of the dining car when the train lurched, and her coffee spilled and wet my sleeve. The baby started crying as we swayed in the aisle, and the mother wiped at my arm with a napkin, trying to sop up the coffee.

The conductor got into the act as well. I waved them off and went back to my cabin, patting my jacket where I'd placed Gennaro's package in my inside pocket. I could feel it tight up against my chest, small and compact. I figured I was carrying about two and a half million euros worth of gems, and the sooner I could deliver them and have the Eurotec people move in, the better.

When I arrived in Prague thirteen hours later, I took a taxi to the address Gennaro had given me and delivered the package. I was asked to wait while the house's occupant, Clouseau, I imagined, verified the contents. I smiled and nodded. *No worries.* The Eurotec guys would be showing up any minute, and I'd be out of there and on my way back to Marina.

That's the last thing I remember until waking up in a cell. It took me a while, but I finally pieced it together. Either the mother with the baby or the conductor switched the package on the train. Or maybe they were in it together. There was no Eurotec posse coming to rescue me, and never had been.

My captors went through my bags and stripped me naked to search me thoroughly. They left my clothes in a heap in a corner and took everything else away. After they were gone, I stumbled over to my clothes and started to dress. That's when I found a scrap of paper stuck deep in my pants pocket. *"I'm sorry. M."* was all it said.

It was Marina, right from the start. She may have worked for Eurotec, and may even have known Nigel. But I'd been an easy mark, ready for the attention of, and sex with, a beautiful and captivating woman. I should have known better, but I didn't. I fell for it. And I thought Gennaro was the twit.

Chapter Six

The leader left me alone in my cell for several days. The knot in the pit of my stomach told me the situation would come to a head soon. Every footstep I heard made me jump and break out in a cold sweat. When they opened the door to leave me food, I'd start shaking all over. I knew if I didn't give up Marina, they'd kill me. It was nothing personal to them, just business.

I was looking out the small, barred window, gazing at the sky and the trees knowing I might never feel the sun on my face again. I turned as I heard the key click into the lock and watched as the door swung open. The leader filled the doorway, backlit by the hall light so that I couldn't read his expression. *This is it. He's here to finish me off.* I knew it, yet I still wouldn't give him her name. I couldn't fathom the thought of her warm, voluptuous body ice cold in death, her animated face as still and waxen as a statue.

"Mr. Donahue," he said my name in a matter-of-fact way that made me shudder as he shifted a small package from one hand to another. "It seems your accomplice has seen the error of her ways."

Her? Did he know about Marina? I didn't understand. Had she double-crossed Clouseau's gang as well as Eurotec and me?

I just stared at him, waiting.

"She has returned our property in exchange for you. There is no longer a reason to make an example of you. But Mr. Donahue, this is not over. Our business with her is not finished. Make no mistake about it. Should you see the lady, please let her know that. We'll be leaving now. And so will you. Two of my men will escort you. Go with them and do not try to return." There was no mistaking the menace in his voice or the promise he made.

I had no words. Marina made a deal with the devil, and he was going to set me free. *Return? Over whose dead body?* Relief flooded through me, then anger. I wanted to strangle Marina for what she put me through. Then I thought of her face and her body, the way she made me feel, and I knew that while I'd never see Marina again, part of me would always be looking for her.

Chapter Seven

I moved back against the truck's side, trying to keep out of the cold wind that brought tears to my eyes. At least I pretended it was the wind. I had to strategize my next move. Without funds or a passport, which the gang had kept along with my wardrobe, leaving the Czech Republic was going to be difficult. The police were out of the question. I'd never be able to explain what had happened or why. And deep down inside, I knew if I went to the cops, somehow the gang would find out, then they'd find me.

Each bump rattled my bones, and each jolt brought a new stab of pain to my bruised and bloodied body.

By the time we arrived at the Farmer's Market in the Dejvice district on the outskirts of the city, my adrenaline rush at being rescued from the forest had ebbed severely, and I was having trouble controlling the tremors taking over my body. My usually steady hands were shaking like leaves in the wind. If the boys at the Chemin de Fer table could see me now, they'd bet the limit and order champagne as they raked in their plaques. The truck ground to a stop, and I mumbled some sort of thanks to the driver, climbed down, and shuffled off into a side alley filled with the putrid smell of the remnants of yesterday's cabbages, onions, and cucumbers. I slid to the ground like a drunk who was on the bender of a lifetime. Tremors racked every inch of my body, and each time I thought they'd stopped, they'd begin again, stronger and more violent than before. I couldn't tell you how long I sat there, legs straight out in front, chin tapping against my chest, shoulders shaking. Just as the sun was beginning to make its way over the edge of the city, I roused myself enough to get up and get moving.

Prague was familiar to me, a place I knew and liked. I'd played at all of its casinos and had won big a few times at the Palais Savarin, one of the city's best. I'd cause quite a stir if I went there now, I thought, looking the way I did. I imagined wandering up the gilt staircase into the old and elegant Baroque building, brushing the dirt from my once-white shirt. "Mr. Donahue," the door concierge would say, "what has happened to you?" and raise his eyes to the frescoed ceiling.

I ran through my options like a poker player, slowly edging out each card in his hand. Not much to work with. Not even a pair of thoughts to parlay into a real plan.

Mentally folding and tossing my worthless deal on the table, I decided to head for the Imperial Charles, a small, discreet, and very expensive hotel in the shadow of the Astronomical Clock in Old Town Tower which rang every hour and rotated the figures of the apostles. A little annoying but in my state my plays were limited.

The manager at the Charles knew me from several previous visits, and I figured I could spin him some tale about my lack of funds, missing credit cards, and passport. "An unfortunate encounter with a young lady's husband," I'd say with a sly wink. "Not a good time to go back to my previous hotel for my luggage, and of course, no need for the authorities." He might raise an eyebrow, but with the promise of a good tip, he'd buy my story and accommodate me.

A few minutes later, I was standing in the lobby, waiting for Josef, the bellman, to show me to my suite. Once inside—and after the shakes had come and gone again—I sank onto the soft down mattress of the four-poster bed and reached for the phone. I needed cash, new plastic, a cell, and most of all, a passport. I knew my banker in Switzerland could get this done in a hurry. He'd better since he was also my younger brother.

Chapter Eight

Alex hated when I played the family card, but really, what choice did I have? I couldn't rake in my winnings and go home; I didn't have any chips left on the table. It was very early, even for an overachieving Swiss banker who didn't keep banker's hours. I'm sure I woke him from dreams of canvas bags filled with fresh, crisp euros sitting on top of softly gleaming bars of gold. You know how single-minded those money-mongers can be.

"Hullo?" A very sleepy voice answered the cell that I knew was on 24/7. As the expression goes: money never sleeps. Especially Swiss money.

"Baby bro, it's me, Nick."

Silence.

I tried again. "Alex, wake the fuck up. I'm in trouble, and I need your help."

When I finally had his attention, I gave him the short version of my tale of woe—the rest would come later when we could speak face-to-face—then I told him what I needed.

"Have my new credit cards, phone, and a stack of euros sent to me at the Imperial Charles by courier, along with your passport and a ticket to Geneva in your name."

"My passport?" I could hear him gulping as he searched

for a reason to turn me down. "Nick, I'm…uh, that's not a good idea…things here are…" He eventually found a rhythm to voicing his excuses. "What about immigration and customs and airport security and using a phony ID? If you get caught…"

He seemed to lose the rhythm as quickly as he found it, and I didn't like the fear I was hearing in his voice. My brother wasn't what you'd call a high-risk taker, but he wasn't a wuss either.

We'd discuss that later as well. "Hey, that's not going to happen." We look enough alike that no one would notice my face didn't match his passport photo. "Listen to me. I need you to do this. Your staid Swiss employers will never find out." I was calculating the odds and betting nothing would go wrong, something I'd been extremely good at until a few weeks ago. "I'll take the first flight out to Geneva in the morning, and you'll have your papers back by noon."

We hung up, and I called down to the desk and asked Josef to come to my suite. Armed with a laundry list—literally—and the manager's okay to put the bill on my tab, he headed out to Debenhams, a British department store in Wenceslas Square. I knew the place fairly well from London, and they'd have the clothes I needed. At least I wouldn't have to wander the streets dressed in only my tidy whities. I, on the other hand, aimed my tired body toward the bath, where I planned to soak away my aches and pains in the deep marble tub that was slowly filling with steaming hot water. Then I'd fall into that enormous bed for a nice, long nap.

Surprisingly, I slept for hours until Josef's soft knock on the door at teatime woke me. My arms were flung above my head as if to protect myself from the bad dreams I knew had crept into my mind while I slept. I had a flash of panic before I realized where I was and that I was safe, the residual effects of my dreams no doubt. When I let Josef into my room, he was loaded down with shopping bags and boxes, topped by a large envelope from Alex, whose courier had just arrived at the hotel.

After Josef left with my tea order for a pot of black coffee and a plate of sandwiches, I shook the contents of the envelope onto the bed. I viewed my shiny virgin credit cards, new cell phone, airline ticket, and Alex's passport, along with a nice thick bundle of euros. I felt much better knowing I was no longer a person without the essentials, especially funds—a gambler's worst nightmare.

While the tables at the Palais Savarin were calling to me and my crisp euros like a seedy bar to a sailor who hasn't been in port for a while, I realized the best way to play things, for now, was to stay tucked up inside the hotel for the evening. Who knew if the gang was tracking me? Although, if they had planted a bug somewhere on me, it was in the hotel's trash bin by now, where my old clothes were festering away.

They could be outside, watching and waiting for me to meet up with Marina. Now, that would be quite a feat. If she were still even on this continent, I'd be extremely surprised.

I shrugged off my apprehension and slipped into my fresh, new Oxford blue shirt, navy pants, and, cream linen jacket—in my business, appearance is important. If you looked like a winner, people treated you like one. I shot my cuffs and checked my reflection in the mirror. Only someone who knew me very well would notice the dullness in my eyes and the tightness around my mouth. Probably wouldn't be a problem this evening. I wasn't expecting to run into any acquaintances in the hotel's dining room, where I was anticipating enjoying a very large Scotch and a very rare steak at a table for one.

Chapter Nine

Early the next morning, I hit Prague Ruzyne International Airport on the run, zipped past a security guard who was half asleep, for which I was grateful, and boarded the flight to Geneva.

As we flew over majestic Mont Blanc and finally landed at Privateport Geneva airport, I let out a sigh of relief. I'd cashed out of Prague alive. When I deplaned, Alex was standing in front of a big black Mercedes parked on the tarmac. An immigration officer stood at attention next to him. He took a peek at my, or Alex's, passport, gave a quick nod, and I was official. Not waiting in line ever for anything was one of the perks of working for the world's wealthiest bank.

I slipped into the roomy back seat next to my brother, and we were off. Alex normally drove a small, red Fiat, and the switch to this gas-guzzling monster with chauffeur seemed a bit strange. I'd noticed it was sitting low on its tires, probably due to its armor plating. Maybe they were expecting some dignitary from the World Bank. I gestured to the interior of the car, "What gives?"

He glanced up at the driver, who was busy navigating the entrance to the Autobahn, and gave an almost imperceptible shake of his head. He leaned over and turned on the stereo system. A Mahler symphony flooded the space. I raised my eyebrows questioningly at this musical choice from someone who worshiped and listened only to The Rolling Stones.

Alex leaned in close and spoke softly. "You're lucky the immigration guy didn't examine my passport." He took it out of my hand and slipped it into his jacket pocket. "I haven't left Geneva for months, and he might have noticed there was no exit stamp. Could have been hard to explain how I was in two places at the same time." He gave me one of his long-suffering looks that I remembered from when we were kids. "I had to call in a favor, but a friend at the airport helped me out. Your replacement passport will be ready tomorrow—another favor by the way." Now, it was the put-upon voice to match the look. "In the meantime, you'll have to stay in Switzerland and try and keep out of trouble." He blanched slightly at the last statement.

Alex was twitchy. Again, not really like him, even with the attitude thrown in. And he kept tapping his fingers nervously on the car's soft leather seat. I got the message and kept quiet. I figured there'd be plenty of time to talk later at home.

The car's engine slipped smoothly into high gear as we shot out of the Privateport and onto the A1. Zero to one-twenty was nothing to this baby that ate up the road like a shark in a school of guppies.

"Who'd you have to kill at SuisseBank to rate such a luxurious 'owto'?" I asked, pronouncing the word with the guttural Swisserdeutch accent and gesturing to the Merc's well-appointed interior.

Alex glanced in the rearview mirror again to make sure the driver was concentrating on the road and not on us before he shrugged off my question and answered very matter-of-factly, "I got a promotion."

Now it was my turn to show surprise. "A promotion? Not something you thought your big brother would like to know about?" We didn't see each other all that often, but we did e-mail and call each other with updates.

"I was busy. I figured I'd tell you when I saw you in person. Not that I expected you'd be dropping by on such short notice." There was just a touch of sarcasm in his voice, reminding me of the brother I knew and loved.

I eased back into the car's soft leather seat and watched the scenery fly past. Alex only lived a few klicks from the airport, and we should have been there by now. "Did you move, too?" I asked as we left the main road and turned onto a winding forest lane bordered on both sides by massive trees.

He nodded slowly, again cutting his eyes toward the mirror before he spoke. "We're almost there."

'There' was a sprawling Swiss chalet like the kind you see in caper movies from the nineteen-fifties. I wouldn't have been surprised to find Cary Grant leaning against the front door waiting for Claudia Cardinale, martinis in hand.

The house was set at the end of a half-mile drive with a view that took in a good part of Lake Geneva. "Very nice," was what I said, while what I was thinking was 'Are you kidding me?' I kept my inner monologue in check and managed to mumble, "Can't wait to see the inside."

I wasn't disappointed. The hallway matched the exterior of the building with old oak beams crisscrossing the ceiling and walls and gleaming wide-plank floors that looked as if they'd been polished a mere five minutes ago. Alex led the way down a wide corridor that ended at a huge living room with massive windows offering a breathtaking view of the lake. He took advantage of my stunned silence to dismiss the chauffeur.

"Thank you, George. We'll be staying in for the evening. Please tell Mrs. Schmidt we'll have dinner in an hour. And bring my brother's bag up to the room next to mine."

"Mrs. who…" I started to say, but a shake of the head from Alex made me hold back my words.

Once George left the room, Alex exhaled deeply, and all the air seemed to seep out of his body. His eyes went dull, and his shoulders drooped, leaving him as deflated as a week-old helium balloon. I had a startling glimpse of how he'd look as an old man. I didn't like it one bit—seeing as how I'd probably look the same. He noticed me staring and made an effort to pull himself together. "C'mon, bro," I could hear the false bravado in his voice. "Let me show you the grounds." From the look he gave me, it felt like an invitation to a high-stakes poker game I couldn't turn down.

Chapter Ten

I have to admit, it was a beautiful place but not the kind of home a junior executive, even at the world's wealthiest bank, could afford on his own.

"Are you going to tell me what's going on here?" I gestured to the house, the grounds, and the three-car garage where I could see a door sliding silently down over the back of the Merc, Alex's Fiat, the poor relation, dwarfed next to it.

"I…" He looked toward the garage where George was exiting by a side door next to a set of stairs that I assumed led to an apartment above.

"Alex."

"No. You first." He turned back toward me, and I could see fear and confusion flash across his eyes. "Then me. What the hell happened to you in Prague?"

As we walked down to the lake's shore, I told him the whole sordid tale of how I was snookered by a beautiful woman in trouble in Venice, the stolen gems, my kidnapping, my release, and finally, my call to him for help. He didn't interrupt, just nodded as I spoke. When I finished, he grabbed my arms and squeezed them tight. It was a huge show of emotion, especially considering we're not the world's most touchy-feely family.

"Now you. Let's have it."

"About three months ago, my immediate supervisor and one of the division's directors, Didier Schneider, was transferred 'effective immediately' to our office in Basel, which in banking terms is like sending someone from New York to Iowa. One minute he was there, the next gone." Alex snapped his fingers with the flourish of a magician disappearing a coin.

"The next morning, his boss, Herr Johann Widmer, our Managing Director, called me into his office and told me I'd be taking over Didier's duties." Alex sighed and shook his head. "This was a really big deal. All of the Directors have been with the bank much longer than me. And they're all Swiss. I just stood there in shock, nodding my head up and down like some dumbass.

"Later in the week, they gave me the car and George and told me I'd be moving into this house." He tipped his head in the direction of the chalet. "Didier had been living here a few years, and it felt odd to be moving into a house that I'd visited often.

Everything of his was gone, all his photos and paintings, his stuff." Alex shrugged. "In some weird way, it was like he'd never existed."

I looked at my brother, really looked at him, and could feel the anxiety that had settled over him like thunderclouds obscuring the sun. I didn't like where this story was going, but Alex was into the telling now, and I didn't want to interrupt.

"At first, I tried to convince Herr Widmer that I should stay in my flat in the city center. But he wasn't having it. He said that the chalet came with my new position and would be more prestigious when I entertained the bank's clients. I had no choice but to agree and convinced myself I might as well enjoy it." He paused to collect his thoughts. "But something about the way Didier just seemed to vanish made me uneasy. "

"People do get transferred, you know," I said. "There doesn't have to be anything sinister about it."

"You're right, and I would have been okay if I'd been able to speak with him. I tried calling Basel a dozen times. He never answered his cell, and the secretary at the bank just politely kept taking messages. Didier and I worked together every day. We weren't "best friends," Alex made quote marks in the air, "but we were good colleagues. It was very out of character for him to ignore my calls. I checked around the office, and no one else has heard from him either."

Alex gazed out over the lake. I waited for him to speak, feeling more apprehensive than I had a few minutes ago.

He cleared his throat and continued, still staring at the lake. A wind had come up, creating ripples and eddies across its surface. "The bank is into something bad, Nick, really bad. I think they took extreme measures to keep it from coming out."

"Extreme measures?" What the hell was he talking about?

"I think they kidnapped Didier, then murdered him to keep him quiet."

Kidnapping? Murder? My brother was floating as many theories as a poker table full of card counters looking to beat the house. Either that, or he'd been reading way too many spy thrillers.

"Listen, I know you're worried about your friend, but Suisse-Bank Ltd. International is the largest bank in the world. They don't do murder. They don't have to. They make money the old-fashioned way—they steal it legally."

I took Alex by the shoulder and turned him so we were face-to-face. His ice-blue eyes were as intense as a pit boss watching a high roller. Scary. "Have you told anyone else about this theory of yours?"

"No." He looked down at his feet as he answered, and I knew he was lying. It was his tell, the same one he'd had since he was a kid.

"No one else?" My tone said I didn't believe him.

"No. I don't know who I can trust, and I don't want to get anyone else involved in this."

Except me.

"There was something else, Nick. Something that made me certain." The fear crept back into his voice.

"What? Kidnapping and murder aren't enough?"

Alex reached into his pocket and pulled out a key. A dull bronze, it was about an inch and a half long with a squared-off top and V-shaped notches cut into one side.

"A key?" I asked. "This is your evidence?" My voice projected the skepticism I was feeling.

"I think it belongs to a secret safe deposit box Didier rented." He turned the key over in his palm, and I could see the number 223 etched into the top. "It looks similar to ours, but it's not from SuisseBank."

"Where did you get it?" I asked. "You said they cleaned out the house and his office. How did they miss it?"

"The day Didier was transferred, I was out of the office at a meeting with one of our clients. When I got back, I was at my desk and reached for a paper clip. My hand closed around it." Alex raised his hand. "It was right there in the holder. Something made me keep it. Later, after they cleared out Didier's office, I worked out that it must have been his, and he left it for me to find. He was gambling they wouldn't search my desk."

A bet that paid off.

Alex wrapped his fingers around the key, and I heard the

resolve in his voice as he continued. "Then Widmer sent me here with George and Mrs. Schmidt to 'look after me.'"

Those quote marks again.

"I know it doesn't seem like it, but they watch me every minute. I think my cell is bugged." I noticed he put it on the hall table when we left the chalet. "And possibly my office here and at work." Sounded like the bank had taken a lesson from every casino I'd ever played in: make sure someone was always watching.

"The bank has become suspicious. I think they believe I found out their secret. And they're right." He shivered even though the day was mild. "I'm in over my head, Nick. I don't know what to do." His hand squeezed tighter around the key.

Maybe my recent ordeal had made me a bit slow on the uptake, but this wasn't adding up yet. "What is SuisseBank doing that would make them murder one of their bankers, a high-level executive, at that?"

"Illegal internet gambling." He spoke so quietly; I had to strain to hear him.

"I'm not sure of all the details, but from the few things Didier let slip and the whispered phone conversations I accidentally heard when I entered his office, I figured out the bank was up to something. After he disappeared and I found the key, I did a little digging on my own."

Great. Alex Donahue, boy detective.

"I asked a friend in the private client group to check some records." His gaze hit his feet again, and I figured that was the person he secretly confided in—the someone he swore didn't exist. "Our list of new accounts didn't make sense. The numbers were coded in a different format than usual, and Didier was listed as Executive Director for each of them. They were all consigned to a limited partnership company offshore in the Dominican Republic. Again, something we never do. I think the bank created a consortium to launder money for any and all comers, a project potentially worth hundreds of millions." He looked me in the eye. "If we can get the information in Didier's safe deposit box, I'll have the proof I need. I'm sure of it."

That we again.

I might not know the ins and outs of international banking, but I was an expert on the kind of internet gaming that Alex was describing, the illegal kind. It was the perfect way for any illicit group, the mob, Chinese Triads, Yakuza, African dictators, cults, Christian ministries, or even governments, to launder money. The profits were huge, and the risks were worth it if you did it right.

The consortiums were as organized as any profitable legit-imate business. The DR, Costa Rica, the Caymans, or the Bahamas—any offshore island was a good place to set up an "office." The consortium depended on "runners"—think bookies in Armani suits—to recommend and introduce bettors, or in this case, most likely investors from the mob, corrupt politicians like the long-departed Saddam Hussein or other terrorist groups. They'd pick a site, set up 30 or 40 computers, then hire local, cheap labor to "write the bets." All conducted over the phone or on the net.

A client used his credit card to establish a limit. Once that was done, the client received a personal code that was his alone. It was the office's way of keeping track of a client's bets, balance, wins, and losses. Every loss carried a ten percent interest fee. And since ultimately most bettors lose, the fees added up to real money.

The problems usually arose when a client wanted to raise their limit. Only the runner—the person who introduced the client to the office—could facilitate this. It was his responsibility to ensure a client paid up. If they didn't, the consequences could be deadly, as a few gambler friends of mine learned the hard way. One had even killed himself over debts he knew he'd never be able to cover. But these were private clients who would bet on anything: sports, elections, what floor the lift would stop on next.

SuisseBank was into something much bigger. If the bank was the office, they were raking in money faster than a croupier at a craps table could rake in the chips. SuisseBank could be taking "bets" from whomever, running them through to launder the money, and skimming a lot more than ten percent. Once the process was complete, the nice, clean cash would work its way back to the client.

If Alex were right, they wouldn't blink over murdering to protect their position. And if they killed once, well what would stop them from doing it again? I'd lay odds if they suspected my baby brother was on to them, he was in real trouble.

"The friend who helped you at the bank, who is she?" I asked.

"Her name is Simone Wellmans," he blurted out before he realized I'd known he'd been lying earlier about not telling anyone else. "I just...I want to keep her out of it." He hung his head. "She's more than a friend, Nick." His eyes bored into mine. "I can't let anything happen to her."

"Nothing will. Don't worry," I said like it was a sure thing. And we all know how that goes.

Chapter Eleven

The next morning my replacement passport arrived by courier from the Embassy. *My little brother did have some pull.* I smiled as I tucked it into my jacket pocket. After a healthy Swiss breakfast of Musli, Alex called out. He explained I'd paid him a surprise visit and he wanted to show me around Geneva. He told George he'd be taking the Fiat and gave him the day off. The same for Mrs. Schmidt. Once we cleared the drive, he used my cell to call Simone and arranged to meet her for lunch.

My mind had been spinning around like a roulette wheel on steroids. The key, no pun intended, was to find out which bank housed the safe deposit box into which key number 223 would fit. We couldn't exactly waltz into every bank in town with me pretending to be Didier. Someone was bound to twig to that quickly. He must have left another clue for Alex. If he hadn't, we were done for.

"Was there anything else of Didier's that you found?" I braced my hand against the dash as we flew along the A1 back toward Geneva. Alex was shifting through the gears like a man possessed, coaxing out every ounce of the little car's power. He must really like this Simone woman.

He shook his head. "Nothing." He turned to me just as we

caromed around a hairpin curve, and I added my other hand to the dash. "The only thing left in the chalet was a small figurine of a watchmaker from Basel. Didier was from a small town right outside, and I figured it was a remembrance." He shrugged. "I found it in a cabinet under the sink in the master bathroom." He finally focused his attention back on the road, and I relaxed my death grip on the dash a fraction. "I decided to keep it… safe. It's in the glove box." He jutted his chin toward the tiny compartment level with my knees.

The statue was unremarkable. A painted porcelain rendition of a classic Swiss watchmaker in an expected pose: a man with long grey hair and a beard, wearing a leather apron and holding a clock in one hand and a tool in the other. I turned it over and read the inscription on the bottom: Basel-23.3-BRC. It could be a sentimental message from a loved one or the clue for which we'd been searching. My money was on the latter.

"Call Simone and cancel lunch. We're going to Basel."

Chapter Twelve

By the time we drove the 183 kilometers to Basel, the banks were closed for their two-hour fondue and sacher torte lunch break. We took advantage of the long lunch hour to stop in the Smilla Café, a small place not far from the French border that Alex knew to discuss the tasks ahead, including figuring out how to put into action the plan we cobbled together over the last few hours.

During the drive, Alex explained the process for accessing a safe deposit box, and I used my cell phone to call Simone and have her search the internet for Basel banks with the initials BRC.

She got back to us within ten minutes, and I put her on speakerphone so Alex could hear the information as well.

"Hullo, Nick," she said in precise English with a charming British lilt. "There's only one bank that matches: Bank du Roget & Cie." I could hear the excitement in her voice as she filled us in on the process we'd be using to access Didier's safe deposit box.

It appeared that at Bank du Roget & Cie, all safe deposit box clients were required to have an account with the bank, as well as the box. Since Didier was tucking away information for a rainy day the way a squirrel stashes away acorns for winter, it stood to reason that he wouldn't use his name and that the account would be a numbered one. Or at least we hoped so.

"We're in luck, gents," Simone continued, and I could hear the soft click of her keyboard in the background. "The bank doesn't require a biometric fingerprint to access a box, just the client's account number and password. We're assuming it's a numbered account, so no name, passport, or photo ID either."

Luck? Guess it depends on your point of view.

If Simone's information was correct, all we needed was the number Didier had created and his password. Then, all one had to do to tap into one's account was present one's self at the bank's reception desk, request one's box, and offer up the required information. Any bets on who that *one* might be?

I thanked Simone and warned her to delete her computer's history. Then I told her to have a very expensive and long lunch on me at Relais de L'Entrecote, one of Geneva's top restaurants. and not to skip their best dessert, their profiteroles drenched in warm chocolate. I didn't want to have her pick up her chips and run, but getting her away from the office right now seemed like a good idea. I had no way to determine if the bank was keeping tabs on her as well as Alex. If they were, she might be in danger, too. I kept these thoughts to myself as Alex guided the Fiat toward Basel's city center and parked a few streets away from the bank's location on Barfüsserplatz.

Now, as we sat at our tiny table in the back of the café sipping lattes, we debated our next move. Well, my next move.

Alex was fairly certain he knew the number of Didier's account: the code Didier used every day to access information at SuisseBank. While the bank's rule was that no employee was to share his or her personal code with any other employee,

Didier had occasionally asked Alex to perform tasks for him that required entering it into the databases. It hadn't seemed like a big deal any of the times Alex used Didier's code, but now he was beginning to believe that his boss wanted to make sure he knew this number and would remember it.

"Fine. Let's presume we have the number for the account. What about the password?"

"I think I might have an idea about that, too." Alex jumped up from the table. He headed toward the phone kiosk at the back of the café. "I want to check the city directory."

While Alex stepped away, I pulled out my cell and made a call to England to my former best friend Nigel, the man who had introduced me to Marina, the cause of my recent troubles. I hadn't forgiven him yet, but I was going to ream him out and then give him a chance to redeem himself in spades.

"My God, Nick! I've been worried sick about you," he bellowed into the phone before I had a chance to speak. One of the dangers of smartphones with caller ID is that everyone knows it's you calling. "Marina rang and told me what happened. Thank God you're okay!"

My stomach lurched, and I thought I might lose the raclette I'd just eaten. "Marina?" I croaked out feebly. "You…you've spoken to her?" I turned and looked over my shoulder, expecting to find one of the Serbian thugs looming behind me. Their leader had warned me about finding Marina, hadn't he?

What was she playing at calling Nigel? I knew she'd tricked him, too. How could she have explained what happened? My hands started to shake as the trauma of the last few weeks came rushing back. What the hell was going on?

"…Nick? Are you there?"

I finally tuned back into Nigel and cut him off before he could go any further. "I'm … fine. That's not why I called. We'll…we can discuss Venice…and…Marina…later." I felt a sharp pain niggling its way into my temples. Not a good sign. Fear or thoughts of Marina couldn't distract me right now.

Put her out of your mind. It's done. She's gone.

I took a deep breath. "Nige, I need your help with something else. Something that could be a matter of life and death."

To his credit, he didn't snort at my dramatic pronouncement. Instead, he listened without interrupting while I filled him in on everything Alex had told me. I outlined our plan to expose the bank's illicit activities and avenge Didier's murder, which I'd become certain the bank had ordered.

"What do you want me to do?" His response was simple and direct, what I had expected.

Being a big wig in The City, London's financial community, meant that Nigel had the right connections everywhere, including broadcast media, Fleet Street, and Internet news services. Getting the information from the safe deposit box to Nigel and then to the media meant we might have a chance to expose SuisseBank and get away with our lives. A slim chance, anyway.

"As soon as we retrieve Didier's information, I'll get it to you in London. Once you have it, just make sure it's the lead story on every network and newspaper in Europe." When the story broke, the bank would be ruined. Legitimate investors would bail instantly and would scamper off to hide their money elsewhere. Investors from the mob and the like who couldn't afford to be exposed would pull what money they could and go into their own form of witness protection until the scandal blew over. Heads might even roll, or at least we could hope so.

"What about you and Alex?" he asked, and I could hear the concern in his voice.

"Don't worry," I said for the second time that day. "We'll be fine."

When Alex returned to the table, he was smiling for the first time since I'd arrived in Switzerland. "Did you find what you were looking for?" I asked quietly, casing the café as he took his seat. I still had a creepy feeling that one of the Serbs would pop up at any moment, wave a gun in my face, and demand that I turn over Marina.

Alex nodded slowly and leaned in close. "The password is Mulhouse." There was no mistaking the confidence in his tone.

"And you know this how?" It was one thing for him to sound sure, but another for me to waltz into Bank du Roget & Cie and give them the wrong password. The security team would be all over me faster than a 250-lb. bouncer on a deadbeat player.

"I remembered that Didier had a cousin living in Arlesheim, a small town on the outskirts near here on the Rhine where he was born." He jutted his chin toward the door. "He talked about her often, and how when they were children, they'd take family trips to this great zoo and botanical garden across the river in Alsace. He said it was his absolute favorite place in the world, and he'd love to visit again."

Alex's voice grew somber, and he stirred his coffee around and around. "I think she is…was…his only relative. I thought her name was Metzler, and I was right. She still lives in the same house. I introduced myself as Didier's colleague and told her that I was in Basel for a few days, showing my brother around. I said I just remembered the park Didier always mentioned and thought you would enjoy seeing it but couldn't recall the name."

"How did you get around the fact that you called her and not Didier?" I asked.

Alex stopped toying with the spoon and looked up at me. His expression became solemn. "She didn't seem to have any idea that he was supposed to be living and working in Basel." He shook his head as if to confirm what he believed all along. "I said I couldn't reach Didier since he was on bank business in Russia, and the cell service was spotty. She didn't question it, Nick. She told me the name of the park and asked me to tell Didier he owed her a visit."

Alex slammed his hand down on the table hard enough to make our silverware jump. A few of the other patrons in the café looked over at us but, seeing nothing too interesting, quickly went back to their conversations. "Let's get those bastards, Nick."

"Count on it," I said as I put my hand over my brother's on the hard wooden table.

Chapter Thirteen

The sun was shining as we left the café and it occurred to me that we could walk down to the river and take a ferry across to France or Germany in a matter of minutes. Alex could escape from the bank, and I could escape from my thoughts of Marina. Or, I could try.

In any event, that was not to happen. As we rounded the corner to Barfüsserplatz, the clock on top of the main post office struck 2:00 PM. Time for my matinee performance.

Alex had made me repeat Didier's account code and password at least twenty times. If I got it wrong, there was no one to blame but myself. I squared my shoulders, lifted my chin, tugged down my jacket, and pushed through massive brass doors into a place where time had come to a complete standstill sometime around the turn of the century, the last century.

The bank was old-fashioned, emphasis on old—fashion had deserted it a long time ago. I walked slowly across the black-and-white patterned marble floors and took in my surroundings. Its high ceilings seemed higher still, lit as they were by dim, hanging globe lights that cast ominous shadows far into the corners. A huge, carved wooden desk faced the main door and was flanked on either side by tall brass plant stands topped by towering intertwined snake plants. *An omen?*

The only things not old or dated were the two beefy security guards with ear-pieces running into their collars and the chic young woman behind the desk. Tall, blonde, and polished, she rose and greeted me with a professional *"Guter tag. Kann ich helfe ihnen."*

She hadn't pegged me for an American right away. This might work, after all. "Good day," I replied in my best nondescript world accent. "Yes, I hope you can help me." I cleared my throat. "I would like access to my safe deposit box."

"Certainly, sir." She switched to English without missing a beat. "Please wait one moment while I call Herr Seger to assist you." She lifted the phone on her desk, and Herr Seger appeared at my side in a matter of seconds. I figured him for mid-fifties, a lifer in a slightly shiny navy blue suit with close-set grey eyes behind round glasses and a pinched mouth that seemed to speak volumes about keeping the bank's money where it belonged.

"Please follow me." He lifted his hand and indicated a corridor off to his right.

We arrived at a small, modern desk stationed in front of a massive vault enclosed by an iron grille. The desk held a monitor with a sign-in screen and a small keypad, which he indicated with a tilt of his chin. "Please be so kind as to enter your account number and password."

This was it: the moment of truth. I thought of Alex waiting outside as my hand hovered over the keypad. Slowly, I entered the account number he had given me and the password, Mulhouse, all the while waiting for alarms to start ringing. I lowered my eyes to my hands, which I folded in front of me to keep steady.

Nothing happened for what seemed like an eternity. Finally, a light on the screen blinked green, and Herr Seger spoke. "May

I have your key, sir?" He held out his hand. I was in.

I followed him past the grille into the vault, which had magically swung open. He put the bank's key into box 223, and I put in mine. We opened the locks and took out the box. He led me to a small room where I could access the contents in private. About a minute later, I was done. I'd opened it, scooped up the packet of papers resting inside, and tucked them in my jacket. Get in and get out, like a swoop on the craps table. Count your winnings later when you were safe somewhere else.

Herr Seger was waiting outside the door, and we repeated the process in reverse. He escorted me back to the lobby, and I started to leave the bank. Not so fast and not so easy.

Just as I reached the front door, I heard the receptionist calling to me: "Sir. Sir. One moment please." She'd just put down the phone and nodded to the two bullyboys flanking her. They began to walk toward me, speaking into their headphones, moving as carefully as lions stalking their prey.

I ignored the lovely young woman and barreled my way out the door onto the steps scanning the street for Alex. No sign of baby brother. Instead, I locked eyes with George, the chauffeur, who was bearing down on me.

Shit! Now what? I flew down the stairs looking left and right, desperate to figure out where to go. Just as I was about to make a run for it, a big, black Beemer SUV pulled up, and the back door swung open. Alex was sitting inside next to a very scared-looking young woman. "Get in." For once, I did as I was told, and the driver sped off, leaving George and the two security guys staring after us.

"Explain," I said to Alex when I caught my breath.

"I can't." He shook his head. "I was waiting, just as we agreed, when this car pulled up next to me. Simone," he dipped his chin toward the young woman next to him, "was sitting back here."

She peeked around Alex and smiled shyly at me. "I told him we had to leave immediately. We were in trouble. Somehow SuisseBank knew what was going on…and …well, they weren't going to allow it." She grabbed Alex's hand like it was the only life raft left on a sinking ship.

"And you found this out and just showed up here," I asked, "with a car and driver?"

"Not exactly." She handed me a note. "This is for you. I went out to lunch, as you suggested, at Relais de L'Entrecote. Thank you for getting me away from the bank." She dipped her head in gratitude.

"And?" I prompted, clutching the letter as tightly as she'd clutched Alex's hand.

"A woman I'd never seen before walked up and joined me at my table. She told me she was a friend of yours and was here to help you and Alex. She knew about the bank's money laundering scheme and Didier's death. I believed her. She explained what I needed to do." Simone looked at me with a mixture of compassion and confusion in her lovely eyes. "Then she gave me the note for you and said you'd understand."

I let my hands toy with the envelope, turning it over and over as the car sped toward the French border, reluctant to open it. Finally, I couldn't resist any longer and slid my finger under the flap. Unfolding the paper inside, I recognized Marina's easy, looping scrawl.

Ciao Nick,

Nigel told me what was going on. Don't be angry with him. Poor baby, he has no clue as to what really happened in Venice or Prague. I don't know why I feel this need to keep rescuing you, but I can't help it. Make sure you get those papers to Nigel. He's quite anxious to help you bring down SuisseBank. You might almost think it's personal.

Be good, mi amor. And try and stay out of trouble. Goodbye.

M

Goodbye? I looked over at Alex and Simone, holding hands and whispering to each other. My brother might have to trade in one life for a new and different one, but he'd have someone to share it with.

Although, not if we didn't get out of here in one piece. No time to feel sorry for myself now. That could come later.

Chapter Fourteen

The Beemer's driver drove like the devil was hot on his tail, taking corners at speed and flying down the narrow, old streets as he made his way toward the Rhine. The SUV flew along the A35 over the river, past the town of Mulhouse, and into France. Once we crossed the border, I let out my breath, which I didn't realize I'd been holding.

A few minutes later, we turned onto a bumpy side road and into the back end of the EuroAirport Basel-Mulhouse-Freiburg.

By my reckoning, we weren't out of the woods yet. The airport, just a few klicks northwest of Basel, while on French territory, was operated by France and Switzerland, with Germany claiming a piece of the action too, hence the three-part name.

Unfortunately for us, the Swiss were in charge of customs. If word of our escapade had gotten to the officials on duty, we'd be hearing sirens streaking up our bums in minutes.

Our driver must have been thinking the same thing. Without slowing down, he bypassed the customs building and took us right to the tarmac and a waiting British Airways CityFlyer, stairs down, the engine revved up. We abandoned the Beemer with the engine still running, and a minute later, we were onboard and taxiing for takeoff.

I peeked out of the porthole just as a half dozen Swiss airport security vehicles, lights twirling and sirens blasting, swarmed toward the plane as it lifted off. I brought my hand to the front of my jacket and patted the envelope I'd retrieved from the bank. It was safe and secure next to the note from Marina, which was nestled next to my crazily beating heart.

We'd made it out, just in the nick of time.

With room for seventy-six passengers, the four of us—the only ones on board—could spread out nicely. Alex took Simone up to the first-class cabin and spent the flight comforting her. Poor girl wasn't used to this kind of quick getaway. Bet she never had to dodge a sloppy drunken gambler stalking her for a stake.

I tried to chat up our driver, but he wasn't having any of it, or me. My questions were met with noncommittal grunts. But I was nothing if not persistent, and I finally got him to reveal we were on our way to Heathrow in London and that Sir Nigel was going to meet us there.

I gave up on conversation and asked the steward for a large Scotch instead—I'd earned it—then closed my eyes and settled in for the two-and-a-half-hour flight to England.

My life seemed to have taken several strange turns over the last few months, and the idea of returning home to London was less comforting than it should have been. I'd always enjoyed my flat in Kensington with its proximity to Harrods Food Halls and the shops on Brompton Road. But the prospect of facing it alone made me feel sad and bereft. *Get over yourself, Nick. No one appreciates a pity party.*

My mind wandered to Nigel and how involved he'd been with getting us out of Switzerland. Of course, that led to thoughts of Marina and the role she'd played in this. The word 'manipulated' came to mind. Maybe I was being unkind, but hey, I think, given the situation, I had a right to be. In any event, Nigel and I were going to have a very long and serious sit down right after we published the SuisseBank information.

The pilot announced out descent into Heathrow, and I pulled myself out of my funk. Most important was to get Alex and Simone out of London and Europe as soon as possible.

There was one person I knew whom I could count on, although I knew I'd have to ante up plenty, and Alex might never forgive me. The moment the plane touched down, I pulled out my cell and called our mother.

Chapter Fifteen

The conversation went like this: "No, Mother, hell has not frozen over…it has not been *that long* since I called you…I am not flat broke and looking for a handout." Well, who tells their mother the whole truth?

After a few more minutes of Mom's subtle banter, I got around to my real reason for calling. "Mom. Alex is dating a lovely young Swiss woman, and he's bringing her to New York to meet you". That got her attention and started another round of questions. "They'll be arriving tomorrow and would love to stay with you." The last was said with as much heartfelt emotion as I could muster. "Alex was hoping you wouldn't mind."

Wouldn't mind? I'd bet the bank my mother was already making plans for the wedding. It would deflect her from asking why the sudden trip. Alex could explain that to her in person.

My baby brother was not going to be happy about the travel arrangements I just made for him. Too bad. Visiting Mom was better than being murdered by a vengeful Swiss banker. Even if just barely.

Next up was to find a nice safe place for Alex and Simone to hole up in overnight. I remembered a small hotel I'd stayed in on one of my first trips to the city, The Gloucester Place Hotel. The rooms were tiny but clean and well-maintained, and the neighborhood was perfect, quiet, and residential. I called and registered them under Nigel's name. By the time I'd gotten all this done, Nigel's car had arrived to fetch us. The man himself was nowhere to be seen. *Coward.*

I had Nigel's driver take me to his office in The City. I found him at his desk, ferociously typing on his keyboard and focusing on several stock tickers rolling across a bank of HD TV screens mounted on the wall. I dropped the packet of damning papers on his desk.

He picked it up with one hand and pushed a button with the other. A young man entered the office immediately. Nigel handed him my envelope and nodded slightly. The man left as swiftly as he entered.

Nigel still hadn't said a word to me. I guess he was waiting for my opening bid.

"Hi, Nige. How've you been?" I spoke as though we just bumped into each other in Hyde Park. "I've been fine, by the way, in case you were wondering." He finally stopped typing and let out a long sigh, then looked up and gave me his best-martyred face. "Unless you count being kidnapped and battling some nasty Swiss bankers."

"Nick," he began.

"Not another word." I held up my hand. "Unless you're going to tell me the absolute truth."

It wasn't a pretty story.

Chapter Sixteen

Marina wasn't a no-good liar, thief, or con artist. She was a very good liar, thief, and con artist, which was fortunate since her real job was with MI6.

"An agent?" I asked with some degree of skepticism.

Nigel nodded and continued. Marina was an investigator in MI6's Anti-Terrorism Squad. Her intelligence, looks, and fluency in several languages added to her appeal to the agency. Her background didn't hurt, either. Her mother was Italian, and her father was an English barrister. She'd grown up in London, spent summers in Siena, and attended university in Paris, majoring in art and economics.

After school, the British Secret Service recruited her, and she quickly moved up through the ranks. Marina had used the last two years to establish herself as an insurance agent recovery specialist—working freelance for Eurotec International—a legitimate company—in their high-end gems sector. MI6 was investigating ties to several terrorist groups who were using European gangs to steal and sell gemstones to enrich their coffers. They had placed Marina with the company.

It was a perfect cover that allowed her to move freely around the continent, investigating high-level jewel thefts and building a case against the gangs' terrorist ties.

Along the way, she'd solved several important cases, dropping subtle hints about the unfairness of her small recovery fees while Eurotec was snagging the lion's share from their big-name clients. Those looking for someone to manipulate will always notice greed, and eventually, Clouseau's gang took the bait. She'd done a few small deals with them prior to Venice, which was where I came in. The gang trusted her at this point—even crooks can be suckers—and the deal was set. Marina told them it was going to be her last job. She was going to take her cut and disappear.

The real plan was for the Double-O boys from MI6 to plunge in and follow Clouseau, who was fronting the job for an Islamic terrorist group in Afghanistan. They were going to nab the leader of the cell, which was working out of London, and offer its members permanent accommodations in His Majesty's prison.

Marina had, in fact, disappeared, then resurfaced briefly to help Alex and me, and now she was gone again. Only this time, she wasn't the one who planned it.

She'd called Nigel from Switzerland and told him she might need his help. She thought someone was following her but wanted to make sure before she did anything drastic.

Drastic? Like, stay alive?

Nigel tried to convince her to let him send one of his people to pick her up, but she refused and told him she'd get back to him in a few hours. That was the last he'd heard from her. The GPS on her phone had been disabled, and there was no way to track her.

Nigel finished his explanation and drummed his fingers on his desk. "Satisfied, Nick?" His tone left no doubt he pegged me as the villain of the piece.

"You think this is my fault?" Did he forget I'd been held captive for weeks, and I was lucky to be alive? Obviously, that didn't count for much.

"We've got to find her before…." He left his thought unfinished.

I sank back into the chair I'd taken when he began. This 'we' business was becoming a nasty habit I couldn't seem to break. "What about MI6?"

"They were none too happy about her trading the gems for you. The packet you were transporting to Prague was supposed to lead them to the terrorists Clouseau was working with. We learned a rival gang lifted it from you on the train. God knows what Marina did to get it back and free you." Nigel paused to sneer at me, "but after Clouseau let you go, he disappeared, and all bets with his jihadist buddies were off." He looked me straight in the eye. "Then, after that debacle, she had the poor judgment to come to your rescue again. You can see why MI6 might be a bit cross with her."

Seriously? Was he kidding me? A bit cross? "You mean they're tossing in their cards and pulling out of the game? Ghosting her after all she did for them? We have to go all in to save her." Now it was my turn to use 'we.'

Nigel nodded.

The bureau that fostered her was leaving her with no chips and no credit to draw on. I stood up, and the chair scraped loudly against Nigel's polished hardwood floor. "Where is she? Who's got her?"

"I wish I knew." Nigel hung his head. "Perhaps Clouseau had a change of heart and got hold of her in Switzerland. Or one of her informers or contacts turned her in for a fat fee."

He was tossing out possibilities. Neither hit me the right way.

"No." I started pacing in front of his desk. "Clouseau got what he wanted. He's probably in hiding to avoid being beheaded by al-Qaida or whatever fringe group he was dealing with, but ultimately, he'll move those gems when he's ready and pay them what's owed if he wants to stay alive." Personally, I hoped they'd find him and tear his heart out. Beheading was too humane.

I stopped musing and faced Nigel, who was still staring at his desk. "Are there any leads? Anything at all?" I knew I sounded desperate. "Somewhere we can start?"

"Just this." He handed me a folded piece of paper.

I opened it slowly, thinking of the note I'd recently received from Marina. *We have something of yours, Mr. Donahue. It's time to ante up if you want it back. We'll be in touch and let you know when and where the game will take place.* My face grew hot as I read the note.

"Bastards." The word caught in my throat as I crumpled the paper and threw it on Nigel's desk. "Let's go find her."

Chapter Seventeen

I t wasn't until I was back in my flat that I realized Nigel had suckered me in and stacked the deck. He knew I couldn't leave it alone—he'd had an ace up his sleeve and played it at the right time—and that the note would be the clincher. Whoever had Marina had done their homework. For starters, they knew I was a gambler. Not too hard to figure out—one or two clicks on Google would do it. But the note, even though it was printed on plain white paper, had made it sound personal. They also knew about my relationship with Marina and counted on the fact that I would come to her aid.

I started to think about whom I'd pissed off recently, other than my mother.

My fellow gamblers were a competitive lot, and I might have beaten one or two of them badly in the past, but it was all part of how we made our living. None of them would seek revenge over a gambling loss or have the means to do so.

There was the Palazzo Ducale Casino and Signor Gennaro, who'd had the poor judgment to trust me. I'd be surprised if his masters had shown any mercy at the loss of revenue that misplaced trust precipitated. If they were the middlemen between Clouseau and the terrorists, they'd managed to screw up royally.

And, of course, there was Nigel, my dear friend from The City, whom I always suspected had connections within the intelligence community. Where did his interests lie? He talked a good game about rescuing Marina, but that could be a ruse, as well.

All this thinking wasn't getting me anywhere. I was exhausted, mentally and physically, and needed a good night's sleep in my bed, which I hadn't seen for well over a month. I climbed in, turned off the light, and tried to do the same with my brain. Eventually, sleep came, and I was out cold until the double beeping of the phone woke me.

"Get up and get the papers," Nigel demanded and hung up. In a fog, I grabbed my jeans from the floor and a ratty old sweater, then headed for the news shop on my corner. I didn't know why I was following Nigel's orders until I saw the *Daily Mail* headline, which screamed at me from half a block away: *'Money Laundering And Murder At Staid Swiss Bank.'* The other tabloids all had similar headlines. *'Big Holes Found in Swiss Bank'* said *The Sun. 'Swiss Bank's Days Are Numbered,'* touted *The Mirror.*

Nigel had gotten Didier's information into the right hands. At least from my point of view. The bank probably had other thoughts on the matter.

I grabbed a handful of papers and skimmed the stories on the way back to my flat and wondered how many heads would roll at SuisseBank and who would be wielding the axe. Thankfully Alex and Simone would be out of England in a few hours. That only left Marina for me to worry about.

Getting back to sleep was impossible, so I brewed a pot of coffee and thought about my odds of finding Marina. Slim to none, my mind whispered to me, but my heart wasn't buying it.

Chapter Eighteen

Nigel and I regrouped later that morning after I dropped Alex and Simone at the airport. He'd requested the MI6 folks to search Marina's flat for anything that might help find her. It felt like a waste of time to me. Marina would have kept the apartment free of anything relating to her real work in case someone caught her out. And I didn't think the people who snatched her would be careless enough to leave prints or clues lying around. It seemed too well-executed for that.

It was going to be a waiting game; for me, that is holding my cards until whoever sent that note decided it was time to ante up.

The days crawled by as I sat and waited for another missive from Marina's captors. All this inactivity was killing me. I was aching to do something. I called Nigel half a dozen times a day to see if he'd heard anything. So far, nothing. Some days I didn't bother to get dressed, just sat in gym shorts slumped on the couch, and brooded. Even dealing a game of solitaire seemed like too much effort.

I read the papers and took some small satisfaction in the fact they were on the SuisseBank scandal with a vengeance. Herr Widmer, the managing director, had been arrested and charged with fraud and conspiracy to commit murder. His boss, Florian Emminger, had fled to his hilltop villa in Monaco while his bank crumbled around him. The Swiss Banking Commission froze SuisseBank assets, and its clients were ready to riot in the streets—they wanted access to their money. Selfish of them, wasn't it? The depth of Herr Emminger's and the bank's perfidy shocked the financial community. *Yeah, right.* The real shocker was that they'd been caught out.

I was waiting to hear those tidy Swiss cops had wrapped things up and extradited Emminger from Monaco. The sooner, the better, if you asked me.

The next day I was pacing around the flat and heard a noise at the front door. I'd been renting the first floor of a restored Victorian on a small street in Kensington with a short flight of stairs up to the front door that opened onto a common hallway I shared with two apartments above.

I jumped up from the couch and ran to the front window just in time to glimpse the back of a man moving swiftly down the staircase. I flew into the hallway, where I saw a manila envelope had been pushed through the mail slot, and threw open the door. When I looked out, the street was empty in both directions. Whoever had been there had disappeared.

I stared down at the envelope lying on the floor. It was ordinary in appearance; about eight by twelve inches, but its presence gave me a jolt. Picking it up by a corner, I held it at arm's length and stared at it for a long time as if it were an artifact from some distant planet that might suddenly burst into flames. My hand started to tremble, and my mouth went dry. The envelope was bare except for my name printed in block letters on the front. I had no doubt it was from whoever had taken Marina. It scared me more than a dealer turning over

Blackjack five times in a row.

Back in my living room, I set the envelope down on my coffee table and considered what it might hold. My imagination ran away with itself, and images of Marina's beaten and bloodied body played across my eyes. When I finally worked up the courage to slide out the contents, I slumped over in relief. Inside was a photo of Marina holding today's *Daily Mail* with the latest SuisseBank headline dominating the front page. As far as I could tell, Marina looked unharmed, but even in the poorly lit photo, I could see the shadow of fear clouding her eyes, and I could feel the bile rise in my throat. A note was scrawled across the bottom: *Be on the south bank of the Thames in front of the London Eye at 9:00 tonight. Come alone, or we'll kill her.*

I had no doubt they meant it, and for one second, I imagined she was already dead, and they'd photo-shopped her face onto an image of today's paper to get me to agree to meet.

The bastards had chosen one of the busiest spots in the city, a smart move on their part, especially since I had no idea whom I'd be looking for among the dense crowd of sightseers that thronged The London Eye, a popular attraction with a birds-eye view of the city. They, on the other hand, could probably pick me out of a police lineup from a block away.

I reread the note several times, hoping to coax something more from the words or figure out who they were and what they wanted. No dice. If there was any hidden meaning in those two sentences, I couldn't find it.

I debated calling Nigel and telling him the kidnappers had finally contacted me. I dialed his number and then hung up before the call went through. No matter what he promised to the contrary, he'd make sure someone was watching me. I couldn't chance the people who had Marina spotting a tail. I'd meet them on my own and figure out what to do from there.

I dressed in all black—shirt, pants, and jacket—which I hoped made me look inconspicuous rather than like a would-be burglar out casing the neighborhood. This was beginning to feel like a really bad Liam Neeson thriller, the only difference being he'd be brandishing a big gun and kicking butt. I, on the other hand, was armed with nothing more than my dim wits and my desire to find Marina.

I left the flat early and took the District Line from South Kensington to Westminster, then switched for the Jubilee Line to Waterloo Station and walked the last few blocks to the London Eye entrance. The whole journey took about twenty minutes, getting me there with plenty of time left to worry.

Nine o'clock came and went, and still, no one approached me. I studied the faces that passed, trying to pick out the bad guys from the regular people. Was that couple strolling hand in hand and stopping to kiss every five seconds on their honeymoon, or a pair of hired assassins? What about the young guy in the hipster gear slouching against the guard rail smoking? Waiting for his girlfriend or anticipating the right moment to pull out a gun and blow me away? I was driving myself crazy, and it wasn't doing Marina or me any good.

By ten-fifteen, I was crossing the road on the way back to the tube, convinced that somehow, I'd blown the meet when a black Cadillac Escalade pulled up in front of me and blocked the way. The passenger door swung open, and a big bouncer type in Armani exited, opened the back door, and nodded for me to enter. It crossed my mind the ride and the guy were both American, not what I was expecting.

The second my head ducked into the back, and I laid eyes on the man waiting there, I knew I'd nailed it.

"You know who I am?" he demanded before my butt hit the leather seat, jabbing an unlit twelve-inch cigar at me.

My head went up and down dumbly before I found my voice. "Ah…yes… Mr…"

He cut me off again, waving the cigar in my face like a Catholic school nun getting ready to rap some knuckles. "Good," he barked. "Make yourself comfortable. We're going for a little ride."

It was a line I had hoped never to hear outside of a movie. Was this really happening again? All I could think about as the car drove off into the night was that, this time no one knew where I was. Nigel would be pissed off royally when he found out I'd taken matters into my own hands. That's if Mr. Tomasso Bonnannaio let me live to tell the tale.

Anyone who'd ever opened a newspaper or watched TV news knew who Tomasso "Tommy B" Bonnannaio was. His close-set, nearly black eyes, crooked nose, and small brush mustache made the head of the New York Syndicate a face hard to forget. I'd heard stories of how he'd clawed his way up the ladder, taking out the competition along the way. This was not a man you wanted to take a ride with, not with all those vowels at the end of his name and the muscle to back them up.

I sat back and tried to review my options as we drove out of the center of the city and headed south. Nothing came to mind. As far as I could tell, my only choice for escape was to hurl myself out of an SUV doing about eighty, and wind up as road kill. That, or sit here and go with the flow.

Tommy B chomped on the end of his cigar and stared out the window, and I did the same on my side of the seat, the staring part, that is. After about an hour, a road sign alerted me we'd arrived in Dorking, a quiet bedroom community within commuting distance of the city. A few minutes later, we pulled up in front of a small two-story pale pink cottage with dormers over the top floor windows. Very English countryside. I would have appreciated it more if I hadn't been so scared.

The big guy came around and opened the door for Tommy, who moved quickly from the car and entered the house. I followed more slowly, still assessing my prospects of escape until Mr. Muscle took me by the arm with one hand, showed me the gun strapped under his arm with the other, and led me down the garden path. Evidently, he'd done this before and had it down pat.

Once we were all settled in front of the electric fire, Tommy B got down to business. "Joey, get Mr. Donahue a drink," he told the bruiser who was now blocking the door. "Scotch, right?" he asked me.

I nodded as Joey went to a sideboard and filled a glass. *My last drink before dying?*

"You know why you're here?" he asked.

It crossed my mind to play dumb, but one look at those bottomless black eyes disabused me of that idea. "Yes." My answer hung in the air between us while he took me in. It wasn't too hard to figure out that this was about SuisseBank and the money laundering they'd been doing for their clients, the New York mob included.

"You and your brother, Alex, you messed up my operation." He paused and lifted his hands skyward. "You understand. I can't let that pass."

Really. Seemed a little selfish.

"You owe me, Mr. Donahue. So does your brother. But since he left town to visit your mother in New York, you'll have to do."

The implied threat toward my family wasn't hard to miss. Neither was the look that said he could grab Alex in a heartbeat if he wanted to. Tommy sat back in the big wing chair he'd taken when we entered the room and watched me. "Your little stunt with SuisseBank cost me, and you're going to get my money back for me."

His money? Was he crazy? Okay, yes, but still, how was I supposed to do that? I just stared at him in disbelief.

"Well, Mr. Donahue?" A flicker of impatience flared in his eyes.

"Not until I see Marina." I jumped up, the words out of my mouth, before I realized I was speaking or that what I was saying might imply I meant to do his bidding.

Tommy raised his eyebrows. "I don't think you're in any position to make demands, do you?" He glanced at Joey, who was still guarding the door, rocking back and forth on his feet, pounding a fist into his palm, ready to take me out at a nod from the Capo. I sat back down and waited.

"Fortunately, I was able to get my business back on track with a new partner, or we wouldn't be having this conversation."

No. I'd be dead instead, feeding the fishes at the bottom of the Thames. I might still wind up that way since he was basically telling me about his illegal activities.

Tommy waved his cigar in the air. "What happens to SuisseBank is no longer my concern. But Florian Emminger, he's another story." Tommy leaned closer to me as though about to reveal his most intimate secret. "The guy doesn't seem to understand his fiduciary responsibility to me. Can you believe that? Seems to think he can just walk away owing me millions. But you'll change his mind, won't you, Mr. Donahue."

The way he said my name made it sound like a life-threatening disease. I shuddered, and his smug half-smile let me know he'd noticed.

Millions? "How do you propose I do that?" I asked, the words sticking in my throat.

"I'm sure you'll work it out," he replied and handed me a thick folder. "A little bedtime reading," he added. "I think you'll find it interesting."

Chapter Nineteen

He left me to sleep on his proposition. Joey showed me to a room on the second floor. It was spartan with a single iron bed and a small dresser in the corner. He ushered me in and then left me with my thoughts. The door was unlocked, probably so I could use the bathroom, we'd passed on the top of the landing. But I wasn't alone. Joey's bigger, uglier brother was sitting in a chair off to the right. My minder for the night.

My nerves were shot. Images of Prague filled my head, and even though I knew Tommy B's twisted plan included keeping me safe and sound for now, worry had invaded every corner of my mind. He'd neglected to mention just how I was going to relieve Herr Emminger of millions of dollars or how many millions for that matter. I didn't think the banker would hand over the cash with a smile and a pat on the back.

When I browsed through the folder, I could see where Tommy B was going with his scheme and where he thought I'd fit in.

It appeared Herr Emminger had a weakness for gambling, for losing, actually. A terrible habit in general and especially bad for a banker who was doing business with the mob. His game was high-stakes Baccarat, where the buy-in was in the hundreds of thousands of dollars. Fine if you were European royalty, an Arab Sheik, or just plain filthy rich. Not so good if you were skimming your stake from Tommy B and the rest of the bank's investors.

Included in my 'information packet' was an elaborate, embossed invitation. It was printed on thick, creamy stock —the kind my mother was probably picking out for Alex and Simone's wedding right now. The flowing script invited my alter-ego, Mr. Roger Moore, to a *Jeu Privé de Baccarat Chemin de Fer* at the legendary Casino de Monte Carlo in Monaco two days from now—Tommy B had watched too many James Bond movies. The favor of a reply was requested by today's date.

The folder also contained a US passport for Mr. Moore and a ticket in this name for a flight out of Heathrow tomorrow. There would be no sense in explaining that Moore was British. Maybe this was Tommy's idea of an inside joke, albeit at my expense.

I also had a reservation for a prestige suite at the Hotel Metropole Monte Carlo. Tommy had thought of everything, except where I'd get the money for this little excursion.

A separate note in the folder listed the other nine players invited to the game. Emminger was among them. I guessed the Swiss cops had missed the boat, or in this case, the yacht, when it came to nabbing him and that his lawyers had kept him out of the tidy Zurich cell I was sure had his name on it. No doubt he would be at the game. And, it appeared, so would I.

"So, what do you think?" my host asked the next morning. We were back in the sitting room. Tommy was at a small table set with a full English breakfast—fried eggs swimming in oil, fatty bacon, sauce-laden baked beans, and greasy tomatoes, the cholesterol-city works—and gestured for me to take the seat opposite. He continued without waiting for me to answer, his question apparently rhetorical. "I took the liberty of replying you would be attending. You'll go into the game as a rich American, Roger Moore, and beat the crap out of him to the tune of ten million."

Ten million. The magic number. Holy crap was more like it.

"What if I lose?" My voice cracked as I asked. I'd not only have to beat Emminger, but all the other players, to make the nut. And Baccarat Chemin de Fer wasn't my game.

"Make sure you don't."

"Won't he recognize me? I am the person who brought down his bank." It stood to reason someone might have shown him a photo or two of me by now. He might even be using it for target practice.

"Figure it out, Nick. Make sure he doesn't know it's you. Do something different." He gestured from my head down to my shoes. I could see he was becoming exasperated with me.

"Couldn't you just send someone," I glanced at Joey, "to threaten…reason with Emminger and get your money back that way?"

Tommy nodded. "I could, but as I told you before, you owe me. And, there's Ms. DiPietro to consider, if you recall."

I recalled only too well.

"She interfered with several other business interests of mine and caused me a lot of problems." He shook his head in disgust. "I had to rethink my operations and relocate some of my personnel."

Was he talking about the gems and Gennaro? Relocate? Probably to the bottom of the Grand Canal.

"Any other questions?"

I had a list, but none that would change his mind, so I asked what I thought was the most important one of all. "Where am I getting the money to buy into this game?" The small print on the invitation had stated players would need currency totaling a half million dollars as ante, a half million on reserve, plus an additional ten percent of the total for the house. Not exactly pocket change.

Tommy nodded to Joey, who was back in his position by the door. He moved to the wall next to the fireplace and opened a safe concealed behind a pastoral painting. I looked over his shoulder and saw a neat stack of American dollars. All I could do was stare.

"It's the cash you need for the game, plus something for expenses. I'll expect it back with what you win."

"Listen, Mr. Bonnannaio." I tried to keep the pleading out of my voice with little success. "Emminger might lose his stake up front and just go home. The other players have nothing to do with this…with you. I'll have to beat each one of them to get your ten million."

He nodded slowly in agreement. "Exactly. I want you to beat them all before you kick his ass. Pick them off one by one until it's just you and Emminger at the table. Let him think he could win. Then you go in for the kill."

Was he fucking kidding me?

"That's what I expect you to do," his voice had changed from almost jocular to something sinister and menacing, "if you want to see Ms. DiPietro again."

"And what if I can't?"

"Then all bets are off."

Chapter Twenty

Joey drove me back to the city and left me in front of my flat. He told me he'd pick me up at 10:00 PM for the midnight flight to Monaco. "And, Mr. Donahue, be ready. I wouldn't want to have to come looking for you."

I wouldn't want that either.

Joey was minding the satchel filled with Tommy B's buy-in money. The plan was to hand it over on the way to Luton International, an airport on the outskirts of London that was less hectic than Heathrow. I had no doubt it was all arranged for me to board my flight, cash included, with no questions asked.

In the meantime, I had a few things to do to get ready.

First on my list was to check in with Nigel. There were several missed calls from him on my cell, and I knew he'd be wondering why I hadn't returned them. Not a good idea.

I lied. Told him I'd shut my phone off, that I couldn't stand the pressure and needed time to decompress. I apologized. Said I knew if he had any information, he would have sent someone around to get me. I apologized again. Promised to leave the phone on and call him if the kidnappers contacted me and not go running off on my own.

Too late for that.

I hated playing Nigel this way, but it was necessary. He couldn't know about Tommy B and his plan to make me the *Ten Million Dollar Man*. Too much was at stake.

Tommy had suggested I change my appearance. That was next on my list. I hit the optometrist's on the High Street and purchased bright blue contacts to disguise my hazel eyes, along with a pair of high-end black Burberry rectangular glasses with clear lenses. Stylish yet not too showy.

Next, I called in to my barber and had my naturally dark brown hair lightened to a dark blond. Fortunately, he had a backroom for this process, and no one I knew witnessed my transformation or humiliation.

Lastly, I called a friend of mine who did makeup for several shows in the West End. I told her I was going to a fancy dress party and wanted to give my face a fuller look to go with my schoolboy costume. I'm not sure she bought it, but she was kind enough to say she'd send around a few cheek lift wedges that I could insert over my upper back teeth. I hoped they wouldn't make me lisp.

When I returned home, I packed my tuxedo, dress shoes, shirt, and props. I was as ready as I'd ever be.

The flight was uneventful. Joey walked me to the gangway, handed me Tommy B's bag of money, and gave me a look that said I better not lose it.

A short while later, I was landing at the Principality's famous airport. Monte Carlo is a spectacular city along the French Riviera that thrives on its reputation for luxury living, and the Hotel Metropole Monte Carlo was no exception. Housed in a palatial Belle Epoch building, my prestige suite on the penthouse floor had every amenity you could imagine, including a

2500 euro per night tariff that matched its oversized grandeur. *It was only money. And not exactly mine, at that.*

I stowed Tommy B's cash in the bedroom safe and left my bags for the concierge to unpack. It was just a little after 2:00 AM, prime time in the casinos, and I decided to scope out the Casino de Monte Carlo, where I'd be playing Baccarat to die for a few hours from now. No slouch in the luxury department either; the Belle Epoque Casino was all gold and gilt trimming with fancy crystal chandeliers in its Grande Salon and a wood and ebony men's club décor in the Salon Privé where my game would be played.

I hadn't gambled here for a while and wandered around the casino, renewing my acquaintance with the place. It was as crowded as Hyde Park on the first sunny Saturday in spring. The Blackjack, Roulette, and Craps tables were full, and it appeared the casino was having a good night.

Eventually, my circuit took me back to the Salon Privé, where I introduced myself as Roger Moore—to the manager, Monsieur Fairmont, who would be overseeing the game. I arranged for him to send the casino's courier service to collect my cash from the hotel for my stake in the game. Players could buy in with any currency they wished to use, as long as it totaled one million dollars. I'd placed the money in a black attaché case and moved it from the safe in my suite to the hotel's safe, where it could be collected at the casino's convenience. Monsieur Fairmont's eyebrows rose slightly at the mention of cash. The usual method was to hand over a cashier's check before the game, probably from a Swiss bank, and the cash idea threw him a bit. Not one to be deterred by hard cold currency, he smiled and said, *"Bien sûr.* As you wish."

After the formalities were out of the way, I asked for a quick look at the seating arrangements for the game. I was anxious to see where I was placed in relation to Emminger. Fairmont seemed hesitant to reveal this information, but a few hundred euros did the trick. Emminger would be sitting in position 5. I would be in 10, diagonally opposite.

I slept late the next morning after a night of fighting off fretful dreams and awoke to a beautiful day in Monte. Despite the sun and azure sky, my mood was dark and gloomy. This might be my last day on earth, not to mention Marina's, if I didn't deliver. I walked down to Larvotto Beach and practiced counting cards while watching the yachts anchored offshore.

The counting was a wasted effort on my part. Baccarat Chemin de Fer at the Casino de Monte Carlo was played with eight decks, which kept the odds fairly even. Creating, dealing, and counting the four hundred and sixteen cards in my head was just too much for my addled brain to take in, even as a diversion.

Lunch at Café de Paris Monte-Carlo a la Salle was a quiet meal of brochettes and the house wine, along with a stunning view of the harbor. Afterward, I went back to my hotel to prepare for the evening.

I called Nigel and was told there was no new news on his end. Of course, I knew there wouldn't be, but I had no trouble sounding stressed and overwrought. All I had to do was think of Tommy B. A nap seemed like a good idea, and I managed to sleep for a while. Our game was set to begin at 11:00 PM. Being as sharp as possible could literally be a matter of life and death.

After a meal from room service, it was time to dress and head for the casino. Contacts, glasses, and cheek lifts in place, I prayed to whatever gods might be listening, turned off the lights, and closed the door behind me.

Chapter Twenty-One

The casino was even busier than it had been the night before. Management must have spread the word a big game was to take place in the Salon Privé. Bejeweled women in Versace, Armani, and Dolce and Gabbana sexy gowns and men in bespoke Tom Ford black tuxedoes were standing three deep along the velvet rope that separated the salon from the rest of the playing floor. Everyone wanted a front-row view. Even in Monte Carlo, a ten-million-dollar winner-take-all game wasn't something that happened every day. Somehow, the crowd sensed blood might be spilled, and they didn't want to miss a drop.

I kept my gaze straight ahead and nodded to the croupier manning the rope. He greeted me by name and unhooked it so I could enter, then turned me over to another croupier who escorted me to my seat, position 10, on the dealer's right. I sat down, and a waitress took my drink order for a double Scotch on the rocks. I was as ready as I'd ever be.

One by one, the other players entered the area and took their places at the large oval ebony table, betting plaques in one thousand, five thousand, and ten thousand denominations stacked in front of them. At one minute to 11:00, only one seat remained empty: position 5. I panicked for a moment, certain that Emminger had bailed and somehow, Tommy B would blame me. Finally, just as the clock struck the hour, Herr Emminger slid into his seat. The game could begin.

Monsieur Fairmont wished us all a good evening, and, starting from left to right, made the introductions. I recognized the names, if not the faces, of several German, Italian, and French businessmen. There was a sprinkling of royals and Saudi Sheiks, as well as two Japanese men who were eyeing each other warily. Fortunately for me, none of the players from my circle were present—not that they could have afforded the tab—or I'd have been in trouble.

Still, when Fairmont nodded toward my chair and introduced me as Mr. Roger Moore, I expected alarm bells to start ringing. Many of the James Bond films were shot here, and I thought the players might figure it out. Instead, they nodded in a desultory way anxious to begin, barely noticing the cat among the pigeons.

I'd supplied my funds in dollars, but the currency of the game was euros. The minimum bet was ten thousand, a hefty sum to me, but pocket change to this crowd. The croupier shuffled the cards, placed them in the shoe, and passed it to the player in position number 1. He would be the 'banker' to start and would determine the bet for this hand, which he set at ten thousand. The banker played against the house, and the objective was to pull two cards that added up to an 8 or a 9, with 9 being a natural, the winning number. The rest of the players at the table bet on the house or the banker and won or lost accordingly.

The onlookers streamed around the outskirts of the salon, oohing and aahing as pots were won and lost and the croupiers raked in the cards with their long pallets. Player number one held the bank for several hands before losing and passing it along to the next player. The game went on like this for several hours, with increasingly large sums of money being bet on each hand. Several players had gone through their buy-in and were working through their reserve funds. Three had already left the game, tapped out, by the time Fairmont called for a twenty-minute break at 1:00 AM.

I was holding my own and was up by a few million—a novel experience for me. Emminger had begun to scowl every time I won a hand, and I thought he might have twigged to who I was. I waited until he returned to the table to make my way to the men's room a few minutes before the end of the break. I splashed water on my face and tried to calm my nerves. *You can do this, Nick. Just stay focused.* Easier said than done, and I nearly jumped two feet in the air when the door opened, and one of the other players entered the room. I nodded at him and left as quickly as possible.

When we recommenced, it was obvious that the two Japanese players, who had drunk about a bottle of Chivas Regal each, were trying to outdo each other in every way they could. If one bet on the bank, the other chose the house. Both backed up their choices with huge bets. Their losses were my gains.

And so it went until there were just four of us left, then three, then two. Then me and you know who. How this had happened, I couldn't tell you. Maybe those gods I'd prayed to were listening. Or maybe it was just dumb luck.

Emminger had the bank and dealt the cards. I looked at him and saw a smug satisfaction on his miserable murdering face. He was sure he was going to beat me and walk away a winner. *Not if I could help it.*

"Your bet Mister Moore," the croupier gestured to me.

I sat back in my seat and assessed the stack of plaques in front of me. Three million, five or six, maybe. Not enough to bring back to Tommy B. Slowly, I raised my eyes to Emminger's, then pushed all the plaques I'd accumulated into the center of the table as though I were accustomed to wagering millions, on one hand, every day. "All in," I said as casually as possible. "Bet on the house."

The croupier looked at Emminger, waiting for his decision.

He licked his lips, then pushed his stack to the center of the table. It made quite a sight, ten million sitting there, and the crowd, who'd grown completely silent in the last few minutes, let out a collective gasp. He turned over his cards: a 2 and a 3 for a total of 5.

The croupier turned over his, a 5 and a 3 for a total of 8.

Emminger had the right to draw one more card to make his 9. My mouth went dry, and my hands began to shake as he slid a card out of the shoe and turned it over. It was a 2. Not enough.

The crowd went wild, shouting and applauding the dramatic conclusion of the game. Emminger pushed back his chair and stood up, looming over the table, glaring at me before he turned on his heel and left the salon.

I'd done it. Somehow, I'd won. I sat there in a daze as the croupier gathered the plaques, and Fairmont offered his hand in congratulations. I looked around at the faces smiling at the newly rich me like puppies begging for someone to adopt them and stopped short when my gaze floated past a man who looked exactly like Nigel.

Nigel? No, It couldn't be. Not here.

"If you'd like to come with me, Monsieur Donahue," the croupier whispered in my ear, "I believe our casino manager has a check for you." I nodded dumbly and rose to follow him, glancing back over my shoulder to where Nigel's doppelganger had been. The space was empty. It was only after I'd taken a few steps I realized the croupier had called me by my real name.

A few minutes later, Fairmont handed me a check for my winnings. "Thank you for playing with us." He winked. "It was a pleasure to have you in our casino."

Something was going on here—had gone on—and I was the last to know. The game was rigged, so I'd win. Only one person could have pulled it off: Nigel. And here I thought I was being so clever, evading his calls, eluding his watchers, and he'd been on to me the whole time. Nigel had put in the fix. *Thank god.*

I exited the casino into the cool early morning air and right into the path of Joey, who was planted on the steps like a giant Botero statue. "Nice job." He held out his hand, and I turned over the check. "You look tired. You should go back to your hotel."

I started to ask about Marina, but he'd already moved away. He was fast for a big guy, especially one who didn't want to answer my questions. I watched Joey disappear into the shadows and hoped Tommy B would keep his bargain to let Marina go. If not, I'd have to find him. Then I'd have to kill him.

Chapter Twenty-Two

Joey's advice notwithstanding, I was too wired to go right back to my hotel. The adrenaline rush that carried me through the game had ebbed, replaced by a surge of anger. I needed to find Nigel and get some answers. Most importantly, to find out if Marina was safe.

The flags along Casino Square rippled as I traversed its dark cobbles searching for my friend, the lights of the casinos ringing it, creating a false brightness I could barely stomach.

Where the hell was Nigel? Fury boiled up through my veins, and I had a sudden urge to stand in the middle of the square and scream Marina's name at the top of my lungs. Instead, I ripped off my fake glasses and pulled the lifts from my cheeks. Then I sat on the edge of one of the fountains like a drunk who couldn't find his way home. My actions had put Marina in danger, and now I dreaded facing the consequences.

I hoped Nigel would be waiting with news of Marina when I finally arrived at the Hotel Metropole, but the lobby was empty save for the night doorman and lone desk clerk. When I asked if Monsieur Phillips had checked in, he clicked on the computer and shook his head. "Non, Monsieur Donahue."

He handed me my key, and I made my way up to the suite. A change of clothes and a jolt of caffeine, then I'd search for Nigel until I found him and my answers.

The elevator pinged open on my floor, and I walked slowly down the hall, eyes downcast, overcome by a sense of defeat that echoed in my slumped shoulders and dragging footsteps.

When I finally reached my suite and looked up, I noticed a "Do Not Disturb" sign hanging from the door. I hadn't placed it there. A jolt of electricity shot up my spine. Two fingers and the door swung open. There she was, in my bed, a white terry robe wrapped around her. It was déjà vu all over again.

"*Ciao, Bello.*" Her voice was filled with desire as she dropped the robe and moved into my arms.

I stood stunned for a moment until her body was next to mine. Then, everything but the feel and taste of Marina faded away. I'd prayed that she'd come back to me.

And she did.

Acknowledgements

Thanks to the Dame of Detection, Level Best Publishers, Verena Rose, Harriette Wasserman Sackler, and my super editor, Shawn Reilly Simmons, for putting Nick Donahue back in the game.

Thanks to the talented Level Best authors who support and inspire me to keep writing my stories. And, thanks to my sibs at SinC NY Tri-State who offer their encouragement and friendship.

To my friends, new and old, I couldn't do this without you. You are always there for me.

And, last but not least, to my family, Paul, Lauren, Mike, and Madison, thank you from the bottom of my heart.

About the Author

Cathi Stoler is an Amazon Best Selling author and Derringer winner. She is the author of the Nick Donahue Adventures featuring professional Blackjack player, Nick Donahue, as well as the Murder On the Rocks Series published by Level Best Books featuring The Corner Lounge Bar Owner, Jude Dillane. and the Laurel and Helen New York Mystery Series. She has written numerous short stories and is a three-time finalist, and winner of the 2015 Derringer for Best Short Story, "The Kaluki Kings of Queens." Very involved in the crime writing world, Cathi is a member of Sisters in Crime New York/Tri-State, Mystery Writers of America, and International Thriller Writers. Cathi lives in New York City with her husband, Paul. Find out more about her at: www.cathistoler.com, or email her at: cathi@cathistoler.com.

SOCIAL MEDIA HANDLES:

Twitter: https://twitter.com/cathistoler
Facebook: https://facebook.com/CathiStolerAuthor
Instagram: https://www.instagram.com/cathistolerauthor/
Email: https://www.cathistoler.com/contact

AUTHOR WEBSITE:
https://www.cathistoler.com

Also by Cathi Stoler

The Murder On The Rocks Mysteries:
  Bar None
  Last Call
  Straight Up
  With A Twist

The Laurel and Helen New York Mysteries:
  Telling Lies
  Keeping Secrets
  The Hard Way

www.ingramcontent.com/pod-product-compliance
Lightning Source LLC
Chambersburg PA
CBHW030437120726

47903CB00003B/1011